BRAVE HIGHLAND HEART

Story by Heather Kellerhals-Stewart
Illustrations by Werner Zimmermann

Stoddart
Kids
TORONTO • NEW YORK

The author would like to thank Kathryn Cole,
who aspires to play the bagpipes.

Text copyright © 1999 by Heather Kellerhals-Stewart
Illustrations copyright © 1999 by Werner Zimmermann

We acknowledge the Canada Council for the Arts and the
Ontario Arts Council for their support of our publishing program.

Published in Canada in 1999 by
Stoddart Kids,
a division of Stoddart Publishing Co. Limited
34 Lesmill Road
Toronto, ON M3B 2T6
Tel (416) 445-3333 Fax (416) 445-5967
E-mail Customer.Service@ccmailgw.genpub.com

Published in the United States in 1999 by
Stoddart Kids,
a division of Stoddart Publishing Co. Limited
180 Varick Street, 9th Floor
New York, New York 14207
Toll free 1-800-805-1083
E-mail gdsinc@genpub.com

Distributed in Canada by
General Distribution Services
325 Humber College Blvd.,
Toronto, ON M9W 7C3
Tel (416) 213-1919 Fax (416) 213-1917
E-mail Customer.Service@ccmailgw.genpub.com

Distributed in the United States by
General Distribution Services
85 River Rock Drive, Suite 202
Buffalo, New York 14207
Toll free 1-800-805-1083
E-mail gdsinc@genpub.com

Canadian Cataloguing in Publication Data

Kellerhals-Stewart, Heather, 1937-
Brave highland heart

ISBN 0-7737-3099-0

I. Zimmermann, H. Werner (Heinz Werner), 1951-   . II. Title.

PS8571.E447B73 1998   jC813'.54   C98-930513-9
PZ7.K44Br 1998

A young child, denied permission to stay up all night for the barn dance,
hides in the hay and discovers magic in her Scottish traditions
and new respect for her father and his bagpipes.

Printed in Hong Kong, China

For the Stewarts of old and new Glenquaich,
especially Roy Alexander Stewart
who played the pipes.
— H. K-S.

For Stephanie Matthews,
one very brave, determined, wonderful
Highland heart
&
Laurie Anne Stockton
who, in tirelessly assisting,
shared the magic of Cape Breton
and the making of this book.
— W. Z.

Whenever my father gets out his bagpipes my brothers go to visit a friend.

"The neighbors will complain," my mother says.

"I'll practice in the shed."

"Shut the windows," she warns.

"My bagpipes need fresh air," he grumbles.

Whenever my father puffs out his cheeks and plays the pipes, our collie dog, Sandy, creeps under the bed. The horses in the barn flatten their ears. The hens cluck and the rooster crows. The pigs dig deeper in the manure pile. The cows kick up their heels and run away. And I cover my ears.

But one special night everyone
listened when my father played his pipes.

All that day I helped — sweeping out
the hayloft in the barn, stringing colored
lights from tree to tree, tossing salads,
baking pies, whipping cream — I did
everything. Without me we'd never have
been ready for the big party. That's what
my mother said. Then my brothers had to
go and spoil everything.

"You can't stay up for the ceilidh," they told me.

"Who says?"

"Everybody. The dancing goes on all night. Little kids get too cranky."

"Not me."

"I'll piggyback you down to the barn for a look," my oldest brother offered.

"I'm staying up all night like everybody else."

"Talk to Mom," was all they'd say.

Later that evening I watched my
brothers getting dressed in their kilts and
fancy shirts and long socks. My youngest
brother's legs looked funny.

"How come I can't wear a kilt?" I
asked Mom, who was braiding my hair.

"Because you're still a small girl."

"But his knees are fatter than mine."

"Don't you like the plaid ribbons I'm
tying in your hair?" my mother asked.

"They hurt. You're pulling them too
tight," I complained.

My father beetled his brows at me.
"Now don't you be forgetting your brave
Highland heart."

But what's the use of a brave
Highland heart when you can't stay up
all night?

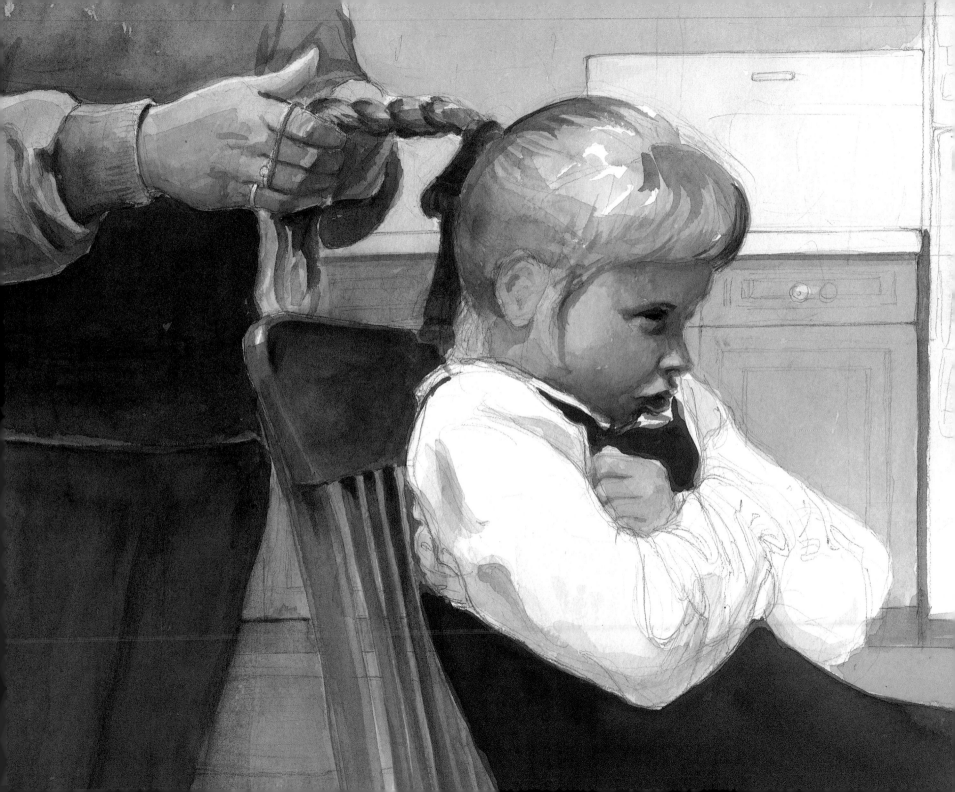

My father fetched his bagpipes.
"I'm going to practice on the far hill,"
he announced.

"Can I come too?"

"Not this time, Little One," my
father said, patting me on the head.
"I have work to do."

My brothers were sneaking out the
kitchen door. "Where are you going?" I
asked them.

"Down to the barn."

"I want to come," I cried.

"No." My mother was firm. "You and
I will welcome the guests."

So the brave Highland heart got to
stand by the farmhouse door watching
all the food arrive. There was baked ham
poked full of pineapple and cherries,
mustard pickles, scalloped potatoes,
little pigs' feet floating in grease, blueberry
scones, rice pudding with raspberry
sauce . . .

Nighthawks began to boom in the darkening sky. Down at the barn the fiddle music started up. The colored lights nodded in the evening breeze — and so did I.

"It's almost your bedtime," my mother said.

"I'm not sleepy."

"You could come down with me for a little while and watch the dancing."

"No. I'm staying up all night like everyone else."

I stomped upstairs and plopped down on my bed. Who cared? I liked being alone. I'd sit there all night, like a screech owl, with my eyes wide open.

Night sounds fluttered at my window screen: a luna moth, bat wings, acacia branches dusting spider webs across the moon's face.

Thump, thump, went Sandy's tail. The front door opened and I heard my mother listening at the bottom of the stairs. Me asleep? Fat chance. The door closed again.

From far away a hen clucked, trying to keep her balance on the roost. The dancers in the barn shouted as they leapt and spun. My brothers too, I bet. And there I was, all alone, in the old, brick house.

Then it sounded — bagpipe music from the far hills, drawing me barefoot down the stairs and onto the grass. I stood there listening until Sandy nuzzled my hand. His nose looked set to sing with the pipes, but I said, "Shh! Not now, Sandy. We can't let anyone hear us."

Fireflies lit our way down to the barn. The night air sang with the pipes. Was that really my father playing as he came down from the hill? I couldn't hear the dancers anymore, or the music of the fiddlers. They were listening too.

When we reached the stable door I told Sandy, "You'll have to wait outside. The horses don't like dogs at night."

Cr-e-a-k, went the old barn door as I pushed it open a crack. King and Queen neighed softly. "Shh," I whispered, pressing my face against their velvet muzzles. "You'll get the other animals started."

I crept up the stairs. The dancers were turned to the sound of the pipes, swirling across the fields. Nobody noticed the shadow sliding over the floor and hiding itself in a mound of hay. Only my head was sticking out. I listened. And the horses and the cows and the pigs and the hens and even the rooster listened. Everyone listened while my father strode to the hayloft playing the long-ago stories.

He was the lone piper sounding the lament as his folk left the glen. On the tall ships that carried them to the New Land, the song of the sea became their music. But my father played on. And when the tall ships touched land, he was there, calling everyone ashore . . .

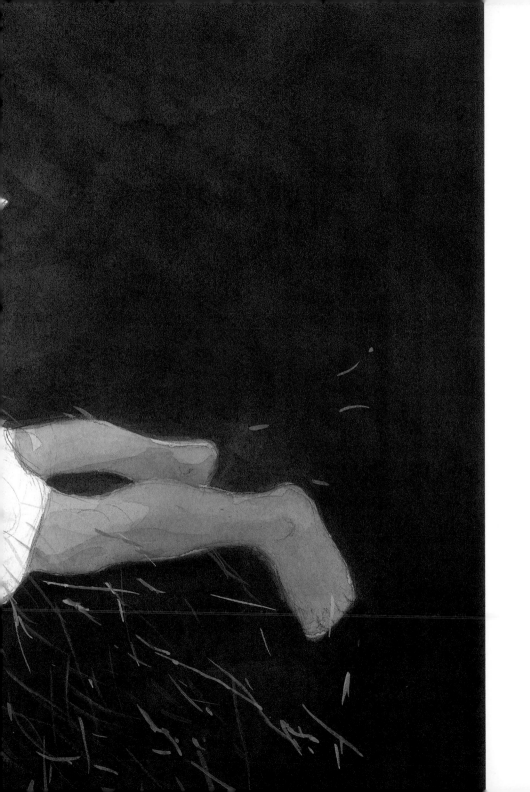

"Aha!"

The bagpipe music stopped. I tried to wriggle deeper into the hay. Too late. My father marched across the floor. "So there's my brave Highland heart."

My father scooped me onto his shoulders and carried me to the middle of the dance floor. "Music!" he called out.

The fiddling started up and we danced, my father and I. My brothers too.
Everyone danced. And if they couldn't dance, they tapped their hooves or
fluttered their wings or thumped their tails.

And the brave Highland heart didn't sleep a wink that night.